Hailey Twitch Is Not a Snitch

Lauren Barnholdt

Pictures by Suzanne Beaky

sourcebooks
jabberwocky

Published by Sourcebooks Jabberwocky, an imprint of Sourcebooks, Inc.
P.O. Box 4410, Naperville, Illinois 60567-4410
(630) 961-3900
Fax: (630) 961-2168
www.jabberwockykids.com

Library of Congress Cataloging-in-Publication Data

Barnholdt, Lauren.
  Hailey Twitch is not a snitch / by Lauren Barnholdt and Suzanne Beaky.
    p. cm.
  Summary: Second-grader Hailey's frustration over a school project releases Maybelle, a sprite whose punishment for being a rulemonger will end when she grants Hailey's wish to have fun, but Maybelle's efforts only seem to cause trouble.
  (pbk. : alk. paper) [1. Rules (Philosophy)—Fiction. 2. Fairies—Fiction. 3. Schools—Fiction. 4. Family life—Massachusetts—Fiction. 5. Massachusetts—Fiction.] I. Beaky, Suzanne ill. II. Title.
  PZ7.B2667Hai 2010
  [Fic]—dc22

                                        2009049937

Source of Production: Versa Press, East Peoria, Illinois, USA
Date of Production: May 2010
Run Number: 12348

          Printed and bound in the United States of America.

              VP 10 9 8 7 6 5 4 3 2 1

For my agent, Alyssa Eisner Henkin,
who never once even thought about
giving up on this book

Contents

Chapter One

- - - - - - - - - - - - - - - - - - - -

French Fries

Addie Jokobeck sits next to me in Miss Stephanie's second grade class. Right now she is moving her pencil up and down and across while we practice our words that begin with *T*. Her pencil is just plain blue. It does not have glitter on it. Or feathers. Or sparkles. Like mine. That's 'cause Addie Jokobeck thinks glitter and feathers and sparkles make your printing wobbly.

"Hailey," Addie whispers. "I think you should be keeping your eyes on your own paper." She smiles at me. Addie Jokobeck is really in love with rules.

"Class," Miss Stephanie says from her big desk at the front of the room. "I have a special announcement."

I sit up and pay attention. I love special announcements, as long as they are not: "Hailey Twitch, please keep your eyes right on your own paper."

"We are going to be doing a special project," Miss Stephanie says. "For School Diversity Week, you will each be making food from a different country, and dressing up as a person from that country. Your parents will be helping you, and you will be working with a partner."

Partners! I love to work in partners! It is like half the work with twice the fun! I quickly look to the front of the room for Antonio Fuerte. Antonio is from Mexico. He told me it is very

2

hot and beautiful there. I try to catch his eye by wiggling my eyebrows up and down and giving him a look. The look says, "Me and you will be partners." My second choice for a partner is my friend Russ Robertson. This is because Russ is very easy to boss. I try to give Russ that same look.

But then Miss Stephanie says, "You will be partners with the person you sit next to in class."

Miss Stephanie is a very good teacher. She has long blond hair and wears lots of dress-up pants. But she is not very good when she is telling me I am going to be partners with Addie Jokobeck who is really in love with rules.

Addie Jokobeck gives me a big wide smile, so big that I can see the space of her one missing tooth on the top.

I raise my hand. "Maybe we should pick our own partners," I say. "That might be fun."

"No," Miss Stephanie says. Then Miss Stephanie says that me and Addie Jokobeck will be doing the country of France.

"Oooh, I love France," Addie says. "That's where French fries come from."

"My grandma has a French poodle," I tell her. "It's a girl dog, but she named it Stewart after my grandpa. It still goes to the bathroom a lot on her rug, even though she's had it for five whole years." Addie looks shocked. "France is not as exciting as Mexico," I say. "It is very boring in France, I think, if the best thing they have there is French fries."

On the way out of school, the meanest girl in room four, Natalie Brice, twirls around and says, "I am partners with Antonio."

"That's nice," I say. Natalie Brice is not my friend because she thinks she is the boss of me. Being the boss of someone means that you are in charge of them. It means if you want them to do something you say, "You are going to do this right now," and they say, "Okay."

"Who is your partner?" Natalie wants to know, even though she already knows the answer to that question.

"Addie Jokobeck, and we are doing France." And then I decide to tell Natalie something else. "We are going to make something very good for our food, like a very delicious dessert with lots of whipped cream out of the can that we will be allowed to squirt as much as we want."

"I think maybe we should make some French fries," Addie Jokobeck says, popping up behind us.

"No," I say, very bossy. "We are making a dessert."

"We are doing Mexico," Natalie Brice tells me. "Only me and Antonio say it like this—*Meh-i-co*. I might even take a trip there with him."

"Me and Hailey say France like *France*," Addie says.

And Natalie Brice rolls her eyes and runs to walk to the bus with Antonio Fuerte.

Chapter Two

Ms. Maybelle Sinclair

When I get home, I am feeling very upset about all this. I stomp inside to the kitchen.

"Hello, Hailey," my mom says. Her hair is in a ponytail, and she is stirring a big pot of spaghetti sauce on the stove. The whole house smells like warm and yummy tomatoes. But it is not enough to cheer me up. "Why are you stomping?"

"Because," I say. "I am very upset." I sit down at the kitchen table.

"About what?"

"Today at school we got put in partners and I have to be with Addie Jokobeck." I show my mom the paper Miss Stephanie sent home with us.

"This looks fun," she says.

"It is *supposed* to be fun," I say. "If you are doing it with someone fun like Antonio, or with someone like your best friend, Russ. Not if you are doing it with Addie Jokobeck." I do not tell my mom that Addie Jokobeck is not fun and that maybe Antonio is going to have so much fun with Natalie making Mexican food that he will forget all about me and our plan to dig a hole all the way to Antarctica. And that maybe Addie is going to ruin the whole thing by making plain old French fries.

"I'm sure Addie will be a great partner," my mom says.

"I am cranky," I tell her. "And I would like to go up to my room, please." When I get cranky, I am supposed to tell people so they will leave me alone until I don't feel cranky

8

anymore. When I forget, I end up having a tantrum or a fit.

A tantrum is when you make a big scene and have a bad temper. Usually I have them when someone is trying to be the boss of me. It starts out by feeling very, very cranky, and then it will keep getting worse and worse until I get my way. A lot of times, I will end up maybe yelling and screaming, or stomping so that my feet make very loud, angry noises. I might even throw myself on the floor and lie on my back, or maybe hide in some racks of clothes if we are in the mall.

"Okay, Hailey," my mom says. "Thank you for telling me you are cranky." She nods and goes back to stirring the sauce, and I go right up the stairs and into my room.

This is not fair! I want to be partners with Antonio because he has black hair and black eyes and on Family Heritage Day he did a special Mexican dance and even taught me how to do it, too. I want to stomp all around my room but I can't because I know my mom will hear me and say, "Hailey, please stop all that stomping around," so instead I go over to my magic castle dollhouse to play—but then I remember that I lost the queen doll who lives in there one time when Russ and I were giving her an operation.

So I pull out the doll of the princess instead.

"I wish I was a princess," I say to her. "And then I would not have to go to Addie Jokobeck's because princesses are very rich and get to have anything that they want." I know this because, one time, I heard my dad say that money can buy

you out of anything. I bet money could buy you right out of a bad partner at school and right into a special partner like Antonio Fuerte. "And then I would be able to have fun, fun, fun, FUN, FUN!"

I decide to put that princess doll back into the magic castle and then go over to my bed and spend some time feeling sorry for myself.

But suddenly, something comes flying out of that castle!

It whooshes right out of one of the castle windows and there is a bright, bright, bright flash of light and then something soft, soft, soft brushes against my cheek. I push it out of the way, but it brushes against me again. And then something that feels like wind is going all through my room! And it pushes me down, down, down to the ground and when I get back up, there is a little person, flying in front of me!

She has sparkly yellow hair and light purple wings and big blue eyes.

"Hello," she says.

Plunk. I am so shocked that I fall right back down onto the floor.

"Oh, no!" the person says. "Are you okay?" And then she flies down to the ground and is

looking right at me. "Did you get hurt? Are you *bleeding? Oh, I am so, so sorry!*" She looks like maybe she is very sorry, too. Not pretend-sorry like sometimes I am when I get into a fight with Natalie Brice.

"I'm...I'm—" I cannot find my voice. It feels like I am trying to talk with a big mouthful of peanut butter sandwich before I've had any milk. My heart is beating very fast in my chest, and I wave my hand through the air, checking for strings from the ceiling that could be holding her up, like maybe it's a trick that my sister, Kaitlyn, is playing on me. But there are no strings. "I'm okay," I say finally.

"Good," the person says. She pats my shoulder. "I think you're probably just a little clumsy." She flies up a little bit in the air, and I stand up, so that we are both at the same level. "My name is Ms. Maybelle Sinclair," she says. She is very small, like maybe as tall as a foot. "And I am a sprite that has come to live with you and bring you some fun!" Maybelle Sinclair holds out her suitcase. "Now where should I put this?" she asks. "You could offer to take it from me. Don't they teach manners here in Massachusetts?"

"Of course I know about manners," I say. We learned all about manners and being polite last year in first grade. Manners that I am good at are bringing my dishes to the sink and being a neat eater. Manners that I am not good at are knocking before going into people's rooms, and not using people's things without asking. Like my sister Kaitlyn's special apple shampoo that can be used as a very bubbly bubble bath. But I am working on it.

"I am Hailey Twitch, and I am pleased to meet you." I put my hand out and wait for a shake.

"That's a little better," Maybelle says.

"Because honestly, you really should—" Then she stops talking and gets a very upset sort of look on her face. "Oh no, no, no!" she cries. *THUNK*. She drops her suitcase on the floor. "There I go, at it again!"

"There you go at what again?" I ask. I sit down on my bed and wait for her to explain. I learned all about patience in first grade, too. It is another thing I am working on.

"Being a rule monger!" Maybelle Sinclair exclaims in a sad voice. She starts zooming all around the room, her long green dress flying out behind her in a long line. She is flying so fast that she almost knocks my whole dollhouse over.

"What is a rule monger?" I ask. I sniff, sniff, sniff the air as she flies by. Something doesn't smell so good in here. I wonder if Maybelle has had a bath anytime soon.

"It's someone who is a stickler for rules,"

Maybelle says. She sighs and then settles down next to me on my bedside table. "Someone who just cannot ever even *think* about breaking rules and wants to do chores. All. The. Time."

"Ohhh," I say wisely. "I know all about a rule monger named Addie Jokobeck." Maybelle raises her sparkly little eyebrows. "She doesn't like glitter pencils," I explain.

"Yes, well, I am not supposed to be a rule monger, because that is how I ended up STUCK IN THAT DOLLHOUSE IN THE FIRST PLACE!"

"Let's use our indoor voices, please," I say, covering my ears.

"I'm sorry," she says. She flies around for a second and then sits down next to me on the bed. "It's just that I've been trying for so long to get out of there. And now I finally am, and I have to remember that I am not going back." She bites her bottom lip. "You see, I am not a very good sprite. I made all the princesses in the castle do their own chores, and I never let them have any fun." She looks very, very, very upset. And then her bottom lip starts to shake, like maybe she might even start crying! "And so Mr. Tuttle, he…he took my magic away and made me live in that dollhouse."

"Is Mr. Tuttle the principal?" I ask. Principals are really not very fun or funny. Mine is named Mr. Jenner and he is very scary with a bushy brown mustache and big gray shoes.

"No," she says. "He…he runs the Department of Magic." Maybelle looks very scared.

"It's okay," I tell her. "You don't have to be scared." I give her a little pat on the back. Then I go and get her some water in my bathroom cup and wait while she takes a long drink. I have to hold the cup for her, of course, because she is too, too, too small to hold it for herself.

"Thank you," Maybelle says when she's finished her drink. "But you don't understand. I have to prove to Mr. Tuttle that I can be fun. Otherwise, I will never get my magic back." Hmmmm. She does not look very fun, with her long dark, dark, dark green dress with long sleeves. Colors that are fun are pink and purple and orange. Not dark,

dark, dark green. But her eyelashes are very sparkly, so maybe there is hope for her yet.

"Okay," I say slowly. I am not so sure about this. "How long have you been in there anyway?"

"I had to wait to get out until someone was really wishing for fun." Maybelle looks at me. "And that has not happened for over two hundred years."

"YOU'VE BEEN IN THAT MAGIC CASTLE DOLLHOUSE FOR TWO HUNDRED WHOLE YEARS?" I yell. Two hundred whole years!! That is longer than anything I've ever heard of even.

"Hailey!" my mom yells from downstairs. "What is going on up there, please?"

"Oh, nothing," I yell back. "Just up here thinking about how not to be cranky."

I wait until I hear my mom go back to the kitchen. Then I decide to be quiet as a mouse.

"You've been in that castle for two hundred whole years?" I whisper very softly.

"Yes," Maybelle says. But Maybelle seems like maybe she doesn't want to talk about that, like when I don't want to talk about certain things, like when something happened last year involving a snowball fight that I didn't even start. "Now, how can I help you have fun?"

I go and pick up Maybelle's suitcase from where she dropped it on the floor. I'm not exactly sure what to do with it, so finally I put it under my bed. Maybe that's where Maybelle will live! Right under my bed! Kind of like a monster. Even though, of course, I know there is no such thing as monsters under the bed.

Then I lean back on my bed and tap on my chin with one finger. I think very, very hard about something fun. And then I say, "Well, there is *one* thing."

"What is it?" Maybelle reaches into the

pocket of her dress and pulls out a teeny tiny black notebook.

"I want to be partners with Antonio Fuerte for our project on all the countries."

Maybelle squishes up her gorgeous sparkly eyebrows. "He is doing Mexico," I explain. "And his grandparents live there on a big ranch with chickens." She does not look so sure. "Mexico is very, very fun." She *still* doesn't look so sure. So finally I say, "If I am not partners with Antonio, I will have to be with Addie Jokobeck and make stupid dumb French fries that people eat every single dumb day."

"Okay." Maybelle Sinclair writes something down in her notebook. I try to read it. But she is covering it with her hand, the same way Addie Jokobeck does when we are taking our spelling tests.

"You are fabulous," I say, clapping my hands. "You can write in cursive and you are not scary at all. And I think I would like to tell my sister about you, please." I take a big deep breath and get ready to scream for Kaitlyn. My mom does not like it when we scream for each other, but this is an exception.

"Shhh!" Maybelle says. She reaches over and tries to clap her hand over my mouth. But it is too small and only covers a tiny part of my lip. "You *cannot* tell Kaitlyn about me."

"Why not?" I ask, pushing her hand away.

"*Because* no one else can see me. Only the person who freed me can, and that's you." She looks at me with a very serious look in her big blue eyes. "And if you tell on me, I will have to go away. I will have to go back to living in that magic castle all the time."

"Okay," I say slowly. "Of course." It is not as fun to have a friend who no one else can see, but it is still fun, fun, fun! And I am going to teach her how to have even more fun, fun, fun.

And we will not be rule mongers like Addie Jokobeck, and maybe I will teach Maybelle to dig a hole all the way to Antarctica just like I was going to teach Antonio!

"Now, Maybelle," I say. "I want you to tell me all about how you were mean to those princesses in the castle and made them do all the chores and would not use your magic and had to get a big punishment for it."

But when I turn back around, Maybelle is gone.

Chapter Three

Maybelle Goes to School

Maybelle is still gone when I go downstairs to have a spaghetti dinner. She is still gone when I leave part of a meatball out on my bedroom floor to see if she is hungry (she's not). She is still gone when my mom comes in to read me a story, and she is still gone when I wake up in the morning.

"Now, Hailey," my mom says at breakfast. "After school today, you will be going to Addie's house to work on your project." And then she rushes out of the kitchen before I can even think about having a big tantrum!

"Ugh," I tell my dad. "I really do not like

Addie Jokobeck." My dad is sitting at the table with me, eating oatmeal. "And that is because I do not think she is very good for fun adventures."

"I'm sure it will be fine, Hailey-bug." My dad takes a big slurp of his oatmeal, which cheers me up right away and makes me laugh, laugh, laugh.

And then Maybelle flies right into the kitchen!

"Good morning, sleepyhead," she sings.

"Where have you been?" I ask. "I have been trying to find you all morning and night!"

"Where has who been?" my dad asks.

"No one," I say as Maybelle swoops all around the kitchen. I cannot talk to Maybelle when my dad is right here. He will think I am craze, craze, crazy.

"Is there a draft in here?" my dad asks, frowning. His newspaper is open on the table, and the pages are blowing around a little bit.

"I don't think so," I say. I hop off my chair and take my cereal bowl over to the sink like I am supposed to. Then I grab my purple backpack off the hook near the door. "Well, see you later!" I say. "Off to the bus stop!"

When I get to school, Addie Jokobeck is sitting in her seat already. Addie Jokobeck likes to be sitting in her seat before school starts, even though we are allowed to walk around the classroom if we want. That is taking being good a little too far.

"Now, where is this Antonio?" Maybelle asks. But I cannot answer her because there are kids around. So I wander up around Miss Stephanie's desk to get some privacy and that is when I see it. The list of all the partners! There is my name, Hailey Twitch. Right. Next. To. Addie. Jokobeck.

"There's the list," I whisper to Maybelle. "Of all the partners." And then Maybelle does something very, very bad. She reaches out, grabs that list, and then smushes it up into a little ball. Before anyone notices, she pushes it down, down, down into the trash can.

"Maybelle Sinclair!" I say, shaking my finger at her just like my dad when he catches me doing something bad. "Why would you do that?"

"Because I am trying to be fun, of course," she says. And then she flies away and disappears before I can stop her.

When it is time for school to start, I sit down next to Addie. Addie's long brown hair is smooth, smooth, smooth. I reach up and try to pat down my blond hair. I forgot to brush it this morning. But it does not matter that my hair is a little messy, because I am wearing pink, sparkly butterfly hair clips that Kaitlyn left in the bathroom. Sparkly clips are better than smooth hair, thank you very much.

"Hi, Hailey," Addie says. She gives me a big smile. "I lost another tooth." Now one tooth on the top and one tooth on the bottom are missing.

I try not to care, but I do. "Did you get any money from the tooth fairy?" I ask her.

"No," she says. "I am going to keep all my teeth forever." And then she pulls out a little cup and shows me the tooth! Addie Jokobeck does not even want the tooth fairy to come! She wants to keep all her teeth forever instead of getting two dollars to spend on candy or glitter pencils or play makeup.

"My mom called your mom this morning," Addie Jokobeck says. She puts her cup of teeth into her desk. "And you are coming over today so that we can figure out what to do about our project."

I am about to tell Addie Jokobeck that I am very busy lately, so she shouldn't get too excited. But before I can, Miss Stephanie says, "Good morning, class! Before we start the day, I'd like to remind everyone of the country they've been assigned for our special project." Today Miss Stephanie is wearing dress-up pants with little stripes on them.

"That's strange," Miss Stephanie says. "I can't find the list." She looks all over her desk. She even looks under her tissue box. But it is not there.

"Miss Stephanie," I say. My hand is shoot, shoot, shooting into the air. "Time to have new partners! I will be partners with Antonio, and you can write it down on a new list! Mexico, please, for Hailey Twitch and Antonio Fuerte!"

"But you and me are partners, Hailey," Addie Jokobeck says. "And we are making French fries."

"You will keep your same partners," Miss Stephanie says. "And I will make a new list." She looks very confused.

Addie Jokobeck grins at me and I can see where her two teeth are missing. I try to smile back, but my lips do not move.

At lunchtime, I sit in my lunchroom seat right across from Russ. And then Addie Jokobeck sits down next to me, even though she was not invited to sit in that seat! Addie is eating a sandwich that has cucumbers on it. Cucumbers do not go on

bread. And they are not
what you eat for your
school lunch.

There is a peanut
butter and jelly
sandwich in my
lunch box. It has
grape jelly, which
I do not really
like. "Antonio!" I
yell down to the other
end of the lunch table. "What
kind of sandwich do you have down there?"

He opens his lunch box to check. "Tuna fish,"
he says.

"Does it have celery in it?" I yell. I do not
like celery with my tuna because it makes
everything all crunch, crunch, crunchy.

He lifts up the bread and looks at his tuna.
"Yes," he says.

"Rats," I say. Usually when I trade lunches with Antonio, he will come and sit by me. And then he will teach me Spanish words, like *perro* means dog, and *loco* means crazy.

"You should not trade sandwiches, anyway," Addie Jokobeck says. "Trading food is not allowed in the lunchroom of Smith Road Elementary."

"Bologna and cheese is the best sandwich to have," Natalie Brice says. She is sitting right next to Antonio with a dumb bologna and cheese sandwich in her dumb purple lunch bag. She pulls off the bread. Natalie Brice has a smiley face made of mustard on her sandwich. "*And*," she says, "the other best thing to have is money for an ice cream from the lunch line."

Natalie Brice knows that I never, ever am allowed to get ice cream from the lunch line! My mom says it is a waste of money to buy that ice cream. And then Natalie Brice says, "I love, love, love tuna with celery in it. Antonio, let's switch our sandwiches."

"Sandwich switching is not allowed in the lunchroom of Smith Road Elementary!" I yell. Then I give Addie Jokobeck an elbow in the side. "Is it, Addie?" But Addie is too busy talking to Megan Miller, who is sitting next to her on the other side. Just when I need her to be a rule monger, she doesn't come through.

So Antonio and Natalie ignore me and switch those sandwiches right away!

"Thank you, Antonio." Natalie takes a big crunchy bite of her new sandwich. "Maybe you can come over tomorrow. And we can talk about our project and maybe help my dad work on the new tree house he is building me."

"Eww," I say, wrinkling up my nose. "That tuna sandwich kind of smells."

"You have a tree house?" Russ asks. He sounds very happy and excited. Also his hair is sticking up, up, up a little bit in the back all over his head. But I do not tell him this, because that is not good manners.

"Not yet," Natalie says. "But I'm getting one." Then she takes her ice cream money out of her pocket and jangle, jangle, jangles it around in her hand. Natalie Brice is very good at being show-offy.

So then I say, "Well, I might be getting braces on my teeth! And you are, too, right, Russ?" Russ and I have a secret plan to put tracks on our teeth. Tracks on your teeth are called braces, and they are very shiny and beautiful. Kaitlyn has them because she is fourteen. My mom says tracks are very expensive. But not if you make them yourself!

But no one is listening. They are all listening to Natalie talk about her tree house.

"Tomorrow I will be working on it with my dad," she says. "It is going to be pink. And have two doors. And a ladder that goes up, and a little window so you can look up at the sky." I chew my peanut butter and jelly sandwich. I try not to think about how if I had a tree house, I would want it to be pink with two doors and a little window so you can look up at the sky.

"So you can come over tomorrow if you

want, Antonio. You too, Russ." But before they can answer, Janie, the cafeteria lady, turns the lights on and off. And we all have to be quiet.

- -

Chapter Four

Tracks on the Teeth

I ride Addie Jokobeck's bus over to her house. I get to have a bus pass and everything! Having a bus pass makes you very important. It means that the bus driver cannot be the boss of you. He cannot tell you that you cannot get on a bus that is not your own, because your *pass* says you can.

Addie Jokobeck has a very fun bus. All the kids are very loud.

When we get to Addie's house, her mom, Mrs. Jokobeck, sets us up in the kitchen and gives us some big books on France to look through. Then she goes in the other room to take care of Addie's little sisters, Delia and Mariah.

"Oooh, look, Hailey!" Addie says. "Here is a recipe for the best French fries ever!" She shows me the book. "Let me see that," I demand. I look real close at the picture. "Those do not look like the best French fries ever. Those look like plain old dumb French fries that everyone eats." I push the book away. "This whole project is a disaster!"

I start to feel very cranky, like maybe I might have a big fit in Addie Jokobeck's kitchen. And then something catches my eye. Something spark, spark, sparkly. Something over in the corner, near Addie's mom's computer. And that is a big, big, big jar of paper clips.

"I think," I say slowly, "that we might need to use those paper clips over there."

Maybelle has been sitting quietly on the chair next to me. She popped right back up when I got to Addie Jokobeck's house. I am still very upset with her for crushing up that list of partners and throwing it away. She keeps saying, "Sorry, Hailey," and, "Please don't be mad at me, Hailey," and, "I was just trying to be fun for Mr. Tuttle, Hailey, so he will give me back my magic." But she did not even get me to be partners with Antonio! That is not fair. And so I am very mad at her.

But when I ask about those paper clips, Maybelle looks nervous.

"What do you need those paper clips for?" Maybelle asks.

I just ignore her.

"These?" Addie picks up the jar and brings it over.

"Hey, Addie," I say, looking at those pink and blue and green and purple and silvery sparkly paper clips. "Did you ever hear of tracks on your teeth?"

Addie Jokobeck is full of surprise and shock. Because she rushes right out to her garage, and when she comes back, she has a big wrench from her dad's toolbox! We can use that wrench to put the tracks on our teeth. Addie also comes up with the great idea of superglue. She might be a little bit good at having fun adventures after all.

Then we go into Addie's downstairs bathroom.

"Now, Addie," I tell her, "you lay out all our supplies on the counter." Addie puts down all the supplies: paper clips, superglue, and the wrench. "Now we have to wash the wrench," I say. "To make it clean. We can't put dirty things in our mouth."

We run the wrench under water from the faucet in the tub. Addie grabs a bar of yellow soap. "I will scrub up this wrench," she says.

"Good," I say. "I'll start cutting the tracks."

But when I try to open the paper clip jar, it won't open! I try and try, until finally, the jar opens and paper clips go flying all over the bathroom.

I giggle. Maybelle picks one of the paper clips out of her hair. She is sitting on the back of the toilet being quiet as a mouse.

Addie grabs a towel off the rack and starts to dry the wrench. "All clean," she says. Then she looks at that wrench very close. "Hmmm," she says. "There are some stains on this wrench that won't come off."

"Let me examine it," I say. The wrench has black grease on it. Some of it is coming off onto the towel Addie is using, but some of it is

not. "Just wipe it off real good." Addie wipes it off real good. She gets some black grease on her white lacy shirt.

"Now," I say, "come here, I need to measure your mouth."

"Me?" Addie looks nervous. "Why do I have to go first?"

"Because I know how to put the braces on," I say. "So you will watch me first, and then you will do it to me." Also, she is going first because I am the boss of her. But I keep my mouth shut about that.

I bend a blue paper clip into half of a circle and slide it into Addie's mouth around the top of her teeth. It fits perfect. "Oh, good!" I say, clapping. "Now that we've done the fitting, we will glue it to your teeth, and then tighten it with the wrench." Addie takes the track out of her mouth so that I can put glue on it.

"Uh-oh," Addie says. She is sounding out words on the package of superglue. "It says 'DO NOT USE ON SKIN.'"

"Teeth are not skin," I tell her. I am hoping that Addie will forget about the rules of superglue for just one minute.

"Maybe you could use this!" Maybelle says from her seat on the back of the toilet. She points to a small pink and white tube on the sink. It says: "DENTURE CREAM." "That would probably work." Dentures are fake teeth. I know all about them because my Aunt Harriet has fake teeth. Sometimes when we visit her on Sundays, they are sitting in a cup of water on her sink.

"Yes, that would probably work," I say. Addie does not notice. She is looking a little bit green. "But I do not feel like helping you to be fun right now, so no thank you." I am trying to give Maybelle a punishment. But I am distracted by that denture cream.

47

"But," Maybelle says, "this is glue. GLUE. FOR. TEETH." I cannot control myself any longer. I need to use that cream!

"What about this?" I ask Addie. I pick up the beautiful pink and white tube.

"That's for when my Grandma Jokobeck comes to visit," Addie says. She shakes her head no, no, no. "I am not allowed to use it. It is for her fake teeth."

"But it's okay," I say. "Because we are *making* fake teeth. Sort of. We need mouth glue and this is it!" I wave the tube around to get her all excited.

"I don't know," Addie says. She does not sound so sure. Probably because she still looks a little green. And also probably because she still loves rules. But I think she just needs to be convinced.

So I open up that tube and smear a big batch of that gooey, gooey cream onto a paper clip.

A little bit gets on the sink. And on my hands. And on the towels. And on the floor. Then we put that paper clip right in Addie's mouth. I hold my breath, and hope, hope, hope that it works. Addie looks in the mirror and smiles big and she has nice, gorgeous, shiny blue tracks on her teeth!

"Do me, do me!" I say, waving the tube of glue in her face. So Addie does me all up with red tracks! And we are smiling and laughing and we have braces on our teeth and it is very fun. Maybelle is so excited by all the fun that she is flying all around.

But then the bathroom door opens, and it is Addie's mom. "Oh, my goodness!" she shrieks. "What have you done to my Laura Ashley towels?!" I don't know who Laura Ashley is, because Addie's little sisters are named Delia and Mariah. But I can tell Addie's mom is mad about the dirty towels.

Then she spots the pink and white tube. And the paper clips. And the wrench. And all of the other gooey mess.

"What is going on in here?" she asks, putting her hands on her hips. Me and Addie don't say anything. We look down at the floor. "One of you better answer me."

Addie's mom is definitely the boss of her.

"Maybe," I say, "it might be time to get back to working on our project."

Mrs. Jokobeck screams, "WHAT IS THAT ON YOUR TEETH?"

And then she pushes us right out the bathroom door, Maybelle flying behind us.

Chapter Five

The Pink Shiny Raincoat

Mrs. Jokobeck got those tracks right off of us with water. But my mom is not happy. On account of the tracks. And on account of that Mrs. Jokobeck thinks I am a "bad influence." I do not know what "bad influence" means. But I do know that it is not good. This is because it has "bad" in it.

So after dinner I am supposed to go to my room and clean it up. I am not allowed to watch TV. I am not allowed to talk to Kaitlyn. And I am not allowed to do anything fun like dance around and practice gymnastics.

"Maybelle!" I whisper very loud. "Where are you?" But Maybelle is gone.

I put some puzzles, my ballet slippers, and
my sand art kit all in a pile on the floor. Then
I use all my strength and push that pile right
under the bed. *Swoosh!* All clean!

And then I hear a noise. A noise coming from
under the bed where I just pushed that pile. It is
a noise with lots of sniffles. Like someone who
is crying and trying for people not to hear it. I
know because I did that kind of crying once at

a sleepover when I needed to go home in the middle of the night. Some people are just not good at sleepovers, and I am one of them.

I get down on the floor and look under the bed. And there is Maybelle! Over in the corner, all smush, smush, smushed up into a little ball.

"Maybelle!" I say. "What are you doing under there?" I know I said that Maybelle should live under the bed, but I really did not mean it. Maybelle cannot live under the bed. That would not be nice.

"I am cleaning up under here," Maybelle says. She wipes her nose on her sleeve. "It is very messy here under this bed, with lots and lots of dust." Then

Maybelle does a very big sneeze. "ACHOO!" But it sounds like maybe she is pretending. She picks up one of the books that I pushed under there. And then she pushes it back out.

"But you do not have a duster," I tell her. I push that book right back under. I just cleaned this room, and now Maybelle is trying to unclean it! "When my mom dusts, she gets out the duster. And some spray dust cleaner that smells like lemons."

"Yes, well, I am going to get it right now," Maybelle says.

"You are going to get what right now?" I ask.

"A duster!" Maybelle says. And then she sniff, sniff, sniffs. Just like I do when I am all finished crying.

"Maybelle," I say very soft, "I think maybe you were having a good cry under there."

"I certainly was not!" Maybelle says. She

flies out from under the bed very, very fast, but I can see that her eyes are puff, puff, puffy. And red, red, red. Also her wings are all crinkly from being smushed up in a ball.

"Maybelle," I say again, "I know all about having a good cry. I've had a good cry lots of times, like when Natalie Brice is mean to me, or when I get punished." I get up from the floor and sit down on the bed. Then I pat the spot next to me for Maybelle to sit. "Now you sit right here and tell me why you're crying. Is it because you feel bad you smushed that list up and I didn't even get to be partners with Antonio after all?"

"No," Maybelle says. Her face is all splotchy.

"Is it because you made me use Grandma Jokobeck's teeth glue even though you knew I wasn't supposed to and you got me in trouble with everyone and now I am a bad influence?"

"No," Maybelle says.

"Is it because you feel bad that a nice girl like me has to be partners with Addie Jokobeck, and not Antonio Fuerte or Russ Robertson?"

"No," Maybelle says.

"Is it because tomorrow—"

"Hailey!" Maybelle says. She holds up one hand so that I will stop talking. "It does not have anything to do with you."

"Oh." I do not know what to say. What else could it be if it doesn't have to do with me? I think very hard. But I am stumped. "Then what is it?" I finally ask.

Maybelle comes up on the bed. She sits down right next to me and crosses one tiny leg over the other. "I'm just upset," she says. "Because I am not very good at being fun. And…and…I am never, ever, ever going to get good at it, and Mr. Tuttle is not going to be happy, and I will never get my magic back! Sprites. Are. Supposed. To. Be. Fun!"

She seems like maybe she is going to cry again. Or maybe have a big tantrum.

"It's okay," I say. I pat her on the shoulder. "You'll learn. Practice makes perfect." Then I decide to tell her this one story I know. "When my sister Kaitlyn started playing the flute, she had to practice, practice, practice." Then I tell her the part that will cheer her up. "And that is because she was the worst flute player in her whole entire school."

"And now Kaitlyn is the best flute player in her whole school?" Maybelle asks. Her eyes look very excited.

"Um," I say. Kaitlyn is only allowed to play her flute in the basement so that the family cannot hear what horrible sounds she makes with that thing. But I do not want Maybelle to know that. "Well, she is still practicing to make perfect." I give Maybelle another good, hard pat.

"I don't know what to do!" Maybelle says. She is on her way to getting very worked up.

"Well," I say. "You might want to start with those clothes you are wearing." I look at her old green dress. "You do not have any fun colors." I point to my shirt. It has glitter butterflies all over it. I do a little dance. "Do you see," I ask, "how these purple butterflies sparkle all over when I dance?"

"Yes," she says.

"That is because this shirt is very fun. When I saw it in the store, I said, 'Now that is a fun shirt. I want it right now!'"

"You did?"

"Yes," I say, "and then my mom

made me ask politely. So I said, 'Mom, may I please have that fun shirt?' and she said okay. Also maybe for Christmas I might get sneakers with wheels on the back so that it will seem like I am roller-skating when I am really just walking." I sit back and wait for Maybelle to be jealous.

But all she does is look confused. "I don't know," she says. "Roller skates for shoes?" She looks down at her feet

"Come on," I say. "I will show you something that will make that dumb Mr. Tuttle very excited."

And then I creep, creep, creep out of my room and tip, tip, tiptoe down the hallway. Maybelle and I tiptoe our way right into Kaitlyn's room. And right into her closet. That is where she keeps her big box of things that she thinks are too babyish but still will not let me play with. There is a doll in there. One that is just about Maybelle's size. One that is wearing a beautiful, pink shiny dress with a glittery sparkly skirt that flows out all around.

"How about this?" I ask. I hold it up for her to inspect.

"I am too old to play with dolls," Maybelle says.

"Not to *play* with," I say. "To wear her clothes." And then I take that pink shiny dress right off that doll and hand it to Maybelle. "That," I say, "is a very fun dress."

I close my eyes while Maybelle changes. And when I open them, she looks very beautiful!

"You look like a whole new woman," I tell her, clapping my hands. "Now twirl around and give me a fashion show!"

Maybelle twirls.

Creak. The door to Kaitlyn's room opens! And poof! Maybelle quick disappears.

"Oh, hello," I say to Kaitlyn when I walk out of her closet. I look very innocent, if I do say so myself.

"What are you doing in here?" Kaitlyn demands. She looks very mad.

"Oh, nothing," I say. "Just looking around."

Kaitlyn looks suspicious. And so I quickly get out of there before she can ask any more questions.

Chapter Six

The Ghost of Room Four

Maybelle is still not back by the next day and I have been looking all over for her! So when recess comes around, I walk around by the schoolyard and call her name real soft.

"Maybelle," I say. "Maybelle, Maybelle, Maybelle, yoo-hoo! Come out, come out, wherever you are!" Then I even say, "I give up, I can't find you!" just in case she thinks we are playing hide-and-seek.

"Who's Maybelle?" Russ asks. He has popped up right behind me. He looks all around. Uh-oh, uh-oh, uh-oh.

"You should not sneak up on people like

that," I tell him. "You are going to give me a heart attack." That is something my Grandpa Twitch says when I sometimes pop up behind his chair and take his hat while he is watching TV. It is a very fun game.

"Who is Maybelle?" Russ asks again. And then he starts yelling, "MAYBELLE, MAYBELLE, MAYBELLE!" And he flaps his arms like he's a bird.

"Shhh!" I say. "Stop that this instant! I do not know what you are talking about."

"Is she that new girl?" Russ asks. "From room five? Where is she? I want to chase her."

"Hey, Russ," I say. "Do you want to go climb on the monkey bars?" This is to make him forget about Maybelle. Russ really loves the monkey bars. He loves to have monkey bar races.

"Okay!" Russ and I run right over to those bars. But when we get there, Natalie Brice is hanging upside down in the middle. Her hair is so long it almost touches the ground.

"Hello, Natalie," I say.

"Hello, Hailey," she says. Then she turns herself right side up. And she jumps down.

"I like your shoes," Russ says.

Natalie Brice is wearing shoes that are roller skates! And she has purple and gold sparkly shoelaces in them! This makes me very, very mad. I am supposed to be the first girl in room four to get those shoes!

"Thank you," Natalie says.

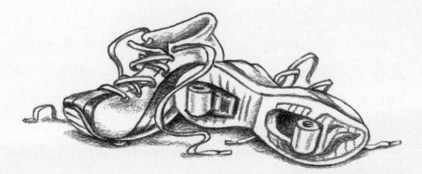

And then Natalie says, "Hailey, what did you think about how Miss Stephanie couldn't find the list of partners?"

"I thought it was very weird," I say. "I have no idea how that list disappeared like that!" Then I give a good laugh, so that she knows I think it is so very crazy. "Ha, ha, ha!"

"Whoever took that list is definitely going to get in a lot of trouble," Natalie says. Then she leans right against the side of the monkey bars. And lifts up part of her foot so that everyone can see those wonderful wheels on her shoe!

"No one took that list," I say. "That list just disappeared. Sometimes things disappear. Like socks in the laundry. Or library books. Or lists of partners." I crouch down in the dirt then so that I do not have to look at those wheels. And then I pick up a stick. I start to write my name, "Hailey Twitch."

But before I even can finish the *H*, Natalie Brice says, "That list did not disappear. Someone threw it in the garbage can."

"Why did they do that?" Russ asks. He is zooming down those monkey bars without stopping even once!

"No, they did not throw that list in the garbage can," I say. I throw my stick down and stand up. "Because Miss Stephanie could not find it. *Poof!* It just disappeared right away!"

I yell over to Antonio who is running around the jungle gym. "Antonio, how do you say *disappeared* in Spanish, please?"

"*Desaparecio*," Antonio says.

"Yeah, well, that list did not just *desaparecio*," Natalie says.

"Yes, it did," I say.

"No, it didn't," she says.

"Yes."

"No."

"Yes."

"No."

"How do you know?" I ask.

And then Natalie Brice gets a little bit of a smile on her face. "Because it turns out that I saw that list. And it was right. In. The. Trash."

"It must have fallen off Miss Stephanie's desk," I say. "And into the garbage. Oops! Like an accident." I smile at Natalie and quick try to make friends.

"Or," Natalie says, "maybe someone threw it in there. Maybe *some* people don't like that list." And then I think she looks right at me. I am not sure because sometimes my imagination runs wild.

Then I have a very good idea. A fab, fab, fabulous idea. An even better idea than the time I made my own lemonade stand and got eleven whole dollars in one day. "Maybe," I say, "a ghost did it!"

"There is no such thing as ghosts," Natalie says. And then she rolls a little bit on her skate shoes.

"Is Maybelle the ghost?" Russ asks. He frowns. "Maybelle is a very weird name for a ghost."

"Yes!" I say. "Maybelle is the ghost!" I try to give Russ a wink. This is what you do when you are joking around about something. But Russ is not looking. He is still zooming on those monkey bars.

And then all of a sudden, before I can stop it, Antonio Fuerte pops right up from behind us. "There is a ghost named Maybelle?" he asks. "Who stole that list?" His black eyes are looking very black, black, black today.

"Why, yes, Antonio," I say before I can stop myself. "That ghost is named Maybelle."

"What does she look like and where is she?" Antonio asks. He jumps up and down and swings his arms all around, like he is pretending to use a sword. "Is she a good witch or a bad witch?"

"She's not a witch," Russ says. "She is a ghost."

"She is a very bad ghost," I say. "She took that list and smushed it right up. But she's gone now, and she said that she is never, ever coming back, so yay for us getting rid of that ghost!" I smile at Antonio. "Now do you want to play chase?"

"I thought we were going to play on the monkey bars," Russ says. He jumps off those bars and into the dirt.

"Oh, yes, we will," I say. I forgot that I am supposed to be playing with Russ. "Sorry, Antonio," I say. "But maybe you can chase me around later."

"I will chase you around and I will stop that ghost at the same time!" Antonio yells. He is really waving his fake sword around now. "I will save you from that ghost, Hailey!" he shouts in a very big outdoor voice. "Her name is Maybelle, and she is queen of the bad ghosts!"

And then before I can stop him, Russ stands up and yells, "GO AWAY, MAYBELLE, YOU STUPID GHOST!"

That is not very nice of him. I am glad Maybelle is not around to hear that. I do not think she would like being called a stupid ghost very much.

"Hey, Natalie, are you glad we got rid of that ghost Maybelle?" Antonio asks. "Since it's a really mean one?"

"Yes, I am glad," Natalie says. "I do not think that ghosts should be allowed at this school." I am very shocked that Natalie is agreeing with me. And for some reason, I am a little nervous, too.

Chapter Seven

The Addie Jokobeck Surprise

Before I know it, the school day is over! We are done with recess, done with gym class, done with everything! And Addie Jokobeck is coming over to my house to work on our French costumes. Me and her are going to give it another try.

"This is going to be very, very fun," Addie Jokobeck says. We are waiting in the classroom for my mom to come and pick us up. "I am so excited to be making a nice costume for France!" Addie claps her hands. Then she bounces all around in her chair. She is wearing white earmuffs that are fluff, fluff, fluffy. And it is not even that cold out.

"Why are you wearing those earmuffs?" I ask her. "When it is not even really that cold out?"

"Better safe than sorry!" Addie says. She smiles.

"Yeah," I say, even though I do not really mean it. I am looking around for Maybelle. She is still not back. I hope she didn't hear all that talk about her being a bad ghost. I don't think sprites really like to be called ghosts. Especially because they are supposed to be fun. And especially ones who have lost their magic.

"What are you looking for?" Addie asks me. "Did you lose your earmuffs?" She looks under the table.

"I did not wear earmuffs today," I say. And then I say, "It is not cold enough." Just in case she forgot.

"Then why are your eyes moving all around like this?" Addie Jokobeck moves her eyes all around like she is looking for something. "If you are looking for your sparkly pencil, it's right here." And then Addie puts her hand into her backpack. She pulls out my pink, sparkly pencil. It is the one with the purple sparkly eraser that matches.

"Where did you get my pink sparkly pencil?" I ask her.

And then Addie Jokobeck's face turns red, red, red. It is so red that it goes up to her ears. It looks exactly like mine when I am caught doing something I'm not supposed to do. "I borrowed it," she says so soft it is hard to hear her.

"Oh." I do not tell Addie that when you borrow something, you need to ask first.

Addie Jokobeck has a weird sort of look on her face. Like maybe she already knows the difference between stealing and borrowing. And then I remember one time when I got in trouble about borrowing. It was last year and it had to do with some wonderful snow boots.

"You know," I say. "I was not even looking for that pencil. I was not even missing it at all. You can probably have it." I put the pencil down on the desk between us.

"I can?" Addie Jokobeck seems very happy

and excited to get that pencil. She is smiling very, very wide.

"Yes," I say. "I have blue and silver and green and gold and lots and lots of pink ones."

"Thank you." Addie takes that pencil. She really holds on to it tight, tight, tight. I think Addie Jokobeck might love that pencil.

"I thought you didn't like pencils with sparkles and glitter," I say.

"Well, I didn't used to," she says. "Because I thought they made your printing and cursive all wobbly. But now I am a better printer, so I think I should be able to handle some sparkly pencils."

And then Addie Jokobeck holds on to that pencil until my mom comes. I think maybe me and Addie Jokobeck might be friends.

"I am going to wear a French mustache," I tell my mom when we get to my house. "So I hope you got some things to make very curly

French mustaches." Then I push my lip up, up, up and imagine how it would feel to have a fabulous, scratchy, curly French mustache up there.

"Oh, Hailey," my mom says, sighing. "I wish you had told me that before. I didn't buy anything to make French mustaches."

I am about to have a fit about this. Because the very best part of dressing for France is wearing a French mustache! But then my mom tells me that we are going to dress up like French painters.

Then she pulls out a big bag and puts it on the kitchen table in front of me and Addie Jokobeck. In that bag are: Some plain white T-shirts. Some paints. And then comes the very best part. We are going to paint stripes on the T-shirts!

We take those white, white, white T-shirts and paint stripes on them with special paint. I love to make a good mess on clothes! And this one is allowed! I make blue stripes on my shirt. Addie Jokobeck paints red stripes on hers.

And then my mom says, "Now it is time for the special surprise."

"I love special surprises!" I gasp.

Then my mom reaches back into that bag. And she pulls out two hats.

"These are special French hats called berets," she says.

I try the beret right on. So does Addie Jokobeck. Those hats are very floppy! They flop, flop, flop right over our eyes.

"*Bonjour!*" I say to Addie Jokobeck from under my beret. *Bonjour* is how you say "hello" in French.

"*Bonjour!*" Addie Jokobeck says from under her beret.

Then we take that special paint and paint those berets right up. I write "Hailey" on

mine in pink paint. And then I put beautiful blue glitter all over it.

Addie writes "Adeline" on hers in red paint. Adeline is Addie's real name. She is just called Addie for short. I am not called anything for short. I think about how maybe I should be called "Hail" from now on. I wonder if that would catch on.

"I love to paint on clothes," Addie Jokobeck 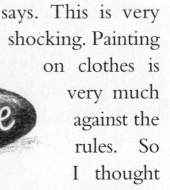 says. This is very shocking. Painting on clothes is very much against the rules. So I thought she probably would not like it too much. That Addie Jokobeck is just full of surprises.

"Do you want to have some ice cream after this?" I ask her. "We have vanilla and strawberries and cream!" Strawberries and cream is the best flavor of ice cream to have. I wait for Addie to get very happy and excited.

"Addie's going to be leaving soon," my mom says. "Her mom is on her way to pick her up."

"Already?" I ask. I feel a little sad in my heart.

"Yes," Addie says. "I am going over to Natalie's to look at her tree house."

My mouth drops all the way open. "You are going to Natalie's?" I am very, very surprised by this. Addie Jokobeck and Natalie Brice are not even friends! Addie is *my* new friend, not Natalie's! And I am the boss of her!

"Yes," Addie says. She is painting stars on her hat.

"You," I say, "should not go to Natalie's. She is very, very mean." I hope Addie Jokobeck knows I am the boss of her. "And I am not invited."

"But her mom called my mom and we are going to work on her tree house and then we are going to have make-your-own sundaes," she says. Make-your-own sundaes! That is the very best kind of ice cream activity! It is very delicious and very messy, two of my favorite things!

I do not think me and Addie Jokobeck are friends anymore. And I think everything might just be a big mess.

Chapter Eight

French Mustaches

Maybelle does not come back until the next day at school. She just poofs right up while we are having free art in room four.

"Where have you been?" I ask her. "I have been very worried about you, like maybe Mr. Tuttle took you away!"

"What do you mean, where have I been?" Antonio asks. "I have been right here!" He is sitting next to me. During free art we are allowed to sit wherever we want. And Antonio picked to sit with me, me, me! I am making a special picture of my family. So far Antonio has taught me that *padre* means father in Spanish, and *madre* means mother.

"I did not say anything," I tell Antonio. "I do not know what you are talking about." I pick up a red marker and draw some lips on my paper. Right on my dad. "Look at these red lips I just drew on my *padre!*" I say. "Aren't those some good lips?"

"Those are some very good lips," Antonio says. He is drawing a picture of his grandparents' ranch in Mexico.

"What is that a picture of?" Maybelle asks. She sits down at the top of my desk. She is wearing her glittery pink dress again. I am going to have to find her some other clothes. I do not think it is good for her to be wearing the same thing over and over again. It will get all dirty. And I do not know how to do laundry, thank you very much.

"This is a picture of my family," I say

to Maybelle. Only I pretend to say it to Antonio.

"I know," he says. Then he wrinkles up his face and looks at me weird. "You already told me that."

"Well, I was telling you again," I say. Then I take the orange marker and make a big sun up in the sky. And I add some purple streaks all around it like a beautiful sunset would look. "That," I say, "is a very beautiful sunset."

"I like that sunset a lot, Hailey," Addie Jokobeck says. She moved her paper over to my art table a few minutes ago. That is because I have been giving her the silent treatment. Addie Jokobeck does not like that.

I pretend that I don't hear her. But Addie does not get the hint.

"I SAID I LIKE THAT SUNSET A LOT, HAILEY," she says.

And then I see something. Natalie Brice is being very, very quiet. She is being quiet the way I am quiet when I am up watching TV and I don't want my parents to realize it is time for bed. That means she is listening very, very close.

"Thank you, Addie," I whisper to Addie so that Natalie Brice will think some secrets are going on.

"You are welcome," Addie whispers back. "And also I want you to know that Natalie's house was not that fun and her tree house is very small." Addie holds up her fingers to show how small it is.

"Really?" I ask.

"Yes," she says. "And also Natalie was asking lots of things about you, like if I thought you maybe threw that list away."

I swallow very hard. "And what did you say?"

"I said no." Addie smiles and shows where her teeth are missing. And I smile back.

"Addie Jokobeck," I say. "I think me and you are friends again."

And then Addie smiles even more.

"Look at my picture!" Antonio says. He is making a new one now. Of a green dinosaur.

"You know, Hailey," Maybelle says, "I'll bet it would be very fun to have a French mustache."

I frown. My mom did not buy the things

for French mustaches. But Maybelle does not know that. She was not in the kitchen when my mom said it.

And then Maybelle does something else. When no one else is looking, Maybelle picks up the black marker. And she draws a big mustache right on her face!

"*Bonjour!*" she says. And she laughs. I did not know that Maybelle knew how to say "hello" in French. And now Maybelle has a French mustache. I start to feel very, very j e a l o u s . Jealous is when you start to want something that someone else has. And I want that French mustache.

So when Antonio is looking down, down, down at his paper, I duck under my desk real quick. And then I crook my finger and Maybelle flies under with me. And then she draws a black mustache right on my face!

"Look at me!" I say to Addie when I pop back up. "Now I am a real Frenchman!"

"Cool!" Antonio says. "I want one, too!" And I can tell by how his black eyes look that he really means it.

"You can't," I say. "You are not doing the country of France. Only Frenchmen have curly black mustaches."

"Hailey!" Addie Jokobeck says from where she is sitting across from me at the art table. "You know we are not allowed to draw on our faces!"

"This is not a drawing," I say. "This is a

French mustache." I reach my hand up and pretend to curl it around my finger. I still see Natalie watching out of the corner of my eye. And so I say, "And you can have one too, Addie, since you are a Frenchman!" So I pick up the marker. "Do you want one?" I ask.

"Yes, please," Addie says. So I draw a nice mustache on her face.

"Drawing on your face is against the rules," Natalie says to Addie. And then Addie starts to look very nervous.

So I quickly hop off my chair and grab Addie's hand and take her over to the sink in the corner. And then we wash, wash, wash our mustaches right off. It is very hard to get marker off of your face. So we must have missed some spots. Because when Miss Stephanie comes around to collect our papers, she sees those French mustaches. And she is not happy about it.

- -

Chapter Nine

Big, Big Trouble

After school I have to go to Addie Jokobeck's house so that we can make our French fries for the party tomorrow.

Mrs. Jokobeck makes Addie go upstairs to change into some cooking clothes. That is because cooking is very messy.

I am already changed into my cooking clothes, and those are my play jeans with a big sweatshirt that used to be Kaitlyn's. It says "I heart NY" on the front of it.

And while I am sitting in Addie's living room, waiting very patient and quietly, Maybelle decides to show up. This time, she is wearing a fancy green dress and green tights.

"Those are very beautiful green tights," I say. "You look just like a beautiful princess."

"Thank you."

Maybelle flies around the living room. "I took them off a doll in room five while everyone was at recess." And then I notice something else.

"Maybelle!" I gasp. "You got your hair done up!" Maybelle's hair is now in flowing curls and ringlets all around her shoulders. It looks very gorgeous.

"Yes," she says. "Do you love it?"

"I love it," I say. "You look very pretty." I reach up and touch my own hair. I think maybe someday soon I might need to get my hair done. And maybe a princess dress like Maybelle is wearing. But mine will be light blue. And I will also have a beautiful sparkly tiara.

"I did it all by myself," she says. "And let me tell you, it is not easy to curl the back of your hair without looking."

"Wow." I jump off of Addie's couch and head over to get a better look at that wonderful new hairdo. "Maybelle," I say, "I think maybe you should be a fancy hairdresser instead of a magic sprite."

"LOOK!" Addie Jokobeck yells. She is all of a sudden in the room. Maybelle screams because she is so surprised to see Addie. "ME AND YOU ARE TWINS!" And Addie Jokobeck is wearing a shirt that says "I heart NY" just like my sweatshirt!

I decide I like being twins with Addie Jokobeck.

When we go into the kitchen, I find out that Addie Jokobeck's dad is very, very fun and funny. He pulls a big chef's hat out of a drawer. And then he pretends that he is a French chef. "Why, hello, *mademoiselles*," he says. *Mademoiselle* is French for "Miss." I like being called "Miss." That is what the lady at the library always calls me when I check out books.

Addie Jokobeck's dad also puts on a fake black mustache! It is all furry and has a sticky back that sticks right to your skin! And he has one for me and one for Addie Jokobeck, too.

"We should all pick out French names," he tells us.

"I will be *Mademoiselle* Hailey," I say.

"That name is not French," Maybelle says. She puts her nose up, up, up in the air. "That is just your own name with 'Miss' in front of it."

"I don't care," I say.

"You don't care about what?" Addie asks. Me and Addie are scrubbing some potatoes in a big pot of water. Scrub, scrub, scrub.

"Um," I say. "I don't care that I am going to get my fingernails all dirty from scrubbing these potatoes!" I drop one potato into the pot, and some of the water splashes up on my face. I laugh and wipe my face off with the sleeve of my sweatshirt.

"How are those potatoes coming?" Mr. Jokobeck asks. He twirls his fake mustache around his finger. "Are they almost ready to be cut?"

"Yes," Addie and I say. Then Addie and I watch while Mr. Jokobeck cuts up the French fries in a special slicer. He puts them into the fryer, and they come out all golden and crispy. Addie and I use big salt and pepper shakers to sprink, sprink, sprinkle them all up.

And then we each get to eat some! I put lots of ketchup on mine, and drag them in a line all over the plate.

"Look, Addie," I say, "these are our French fries and we are dragging them through a bloodbath!"

"And now I am eating the bloodbath!" And then Addie Jokobeck takes a whole handful of French fries and ketchup and shoves it right in her mouth! And ketchup and salt is all over her mouth and even dripping down onto her shirt! I am so shocked that I cannot move for one second. Addie Jokobeck is being very naughty and it is her idea! She is not obeying the rules like she is supposed to!

"That," Maybelle says, "seems very, very

fun." And then, when Addie is not looking, Maybelle picks a French fry right off the tray and throws it at Addie Jokobeck's head! I am shocked for one minute. And I think that maybe Addie Jokobeck is going to be upset.

"You threw a French fry at me," she says slowly. She pulls it out of her hair.

"Yes," I say, even though it was really Maybelle.

Then Addie Jokobeck does something even worse. She squishes up a big handful of French fries and yells, "Food fight!" And then Addie and I are throwing French fries all over the

place at each other and laughing and giggling and ketchup is everywhere! And Maybelle is swooping around and throwing French fries when Addie is not looking and it is very fun, fun, fun and also a big mess, mess, mess.

"Oh, my goodness," Mr. Jokobeck says when he sees us. "I guess you two have decided to take these French fries and turn them into mashed potatoes!"

And he is not even mad! He just helps us clean up.

But the fun does not last long. Because the phone rings while Addie and I are cleaning up our big mess.

Addie Jokobeck's dad answers. And me and Addie hear him say, "Oh, hello, Miss Stephanie." And then he starts talking in a very serious voice. He says, "No, no, she didn't... yes...yes, okay, Miss Stephanie."

And Addie Jokobeck is starting to look very

upset. When her dad hangs up the phone, he says, "Please come into the living room for a moment, Adeline."

So I sit in the kitchen by myself. And when Addie comes back, she has a very sad look on her face.

"Hailey," she says. "I am in a lot of trouble for drawing that French mustache on my face today."

"That's horrible," I say. "Did you get a bad punishment?"

"Yes," she says. "I did." And then she looks at me and takes one big breath. "I am sorry, Hailey, but I cannot be your friend anymore."

"Why not?" I ask.

"Because I am always getting in trouble with you!" Addie yells. "You made me use Grandma Jokobeck's special teeth cream and you will not let me be friends with Natalie and now you got me in big trouble for a French mustache!"

My throat starts to feel very hot, and my heart starts to feel very sad. "I'm sorry," I say to Addie.

But she just turns around and goes to her room. And I have to sit there in the kitchen until my mom comes to get me. But I only cry a little.

Miss Stephanie called my mom, too. She tells me in the car. And now I have to have a special meeting with my parents after dinner. It is not going to be fun or funny or *anything*.

"Maybelle!" I say when I get home from Addie's. I hang my coat on the hook by the door and make sure no one is around to hear me.

"*Bonjour!*" Maybelle says. She spins all around in her new green dress.

"Maybelle, you got me in trouble again!" I say. I stamp my foot so that she knows this is very serious business. "And Miss Stephanie called my mom and Addie's dad and they are very mad and you better stop it, young lady!"

"I am trying to be fun," Maybelle says. "Isn't getting a mustache on your face fun?"

"Ye-esss," I say slowly. "But you keep. Getting. Me. In. Trouble!"

"Who are you talking to?" Kaitlyn asks. She walks into the kitchen. She takes an orange out of the refrigerator and looks at me real strange.

"No one," I say quickly. And Maybelle disappears.

But Kaitlyn is giving me a weird look, like maybe she does not believe me.

- -

After dinner, I have a special family meeting with my parents. The special family meeting is just me and those two. We sit around the kitchen table. Me, my mom, and my dad.

"Hailey," my mom says. "We need to discuss your behavior at school lately."

"No, thank you," I say. "I do not really feel

like discussing that right now." I make a big yawn and a big stretch. "I am mostly just ready for bed. I am so sleepy!" I am not really that sleepy. But I would rather be in a nice warm bed than having a special family meeting.

"Hailey, it's not your bedtime yet," my mom says.

"But getting some good rest is important for school the next day," I tell her. "That is what you always tell me." I think about this. "And having a good breakfast is important, too. Like oatmeal, right, Dad?"

"Yes," my dad says. "That is true about the oatmeal, but this is important, too." He is using a very serious voice with me that I do not like. Not even one little bit. It sounds exactly like the voice Addie Jokobeck's dad used when he called her Adeline and made her go into the living room for a talk.

"Then can I at least have some ice cream

while we talk about this?" I ask. I did not get any dessert tonight because Maybelle ate mine. We had ice cream sandwiches.

"You already had an ice cream sandwich," my mom says.

"Fine." I kick at the table. I am starting to feel very cranky. "I'm starting to feel very cranky!" I announce. "I think I should probably be left alone so that I do not have a bad tantrum or fit."

"Hailey, we need to talk about this," my mom says. "We can't have you getting into so much trouble in school and with your friends."

"I'm not trying to," I say. This is not even a lie. It is only the truth. I am not trying to. *Maybelle* is trying to.

"Well, you need to make sure that it doesn't happen again," my mom says. "I cannot get any more calls at work about how you're acting up at school."

"Oh, you won't," I say.

"Do you promise?" my mom asks.

"I promise," I say. And then I even cross my heart.

"Okay," my mom says. She gives me a hug. And then so does my dad.

But Addie Jokobeck still does not want to be my friend. And that is very sad.

Chapter Ten

Party Time

The next day is the day of the Countries of the World Party in room four! But my mood is ruined because Natalie Brice brings invitations to school. Invitations that are made out of white construction paper and are in the shape of a ghost with big, wide, creepy mouths.

"Here you go," she says, giving one to Antonio while we are all on the playground for recess.

Antonio reads it, sounding out all the words. "You are invited," he says, "to Natalie's Ghost Hunting Party."

A ghost hunting party! Everyone will be

running through Natalie's house looking for that ghost! Of course, I know there really is no ghost. That ghost is really Maybelle. But they do not know that! I could catch that ghost and make them all think it was me who saved the day!

"Here you go, Russ," Natalie says. And she gives him one of those shiny, shiny, shiny invitations. Then Natalie Brice walks right by me and over to Megan Miller and Addie Jokobeck. And I realize I will not be going to that party. For definite.

"Natalie does not have very good listening skills," I say to Russ. "She didn't listen when we told her we already got rid of that ghost by the monkey bars."

"Yeah," Russ says. He is still looking at that invitation.

"So her party is not even a real ghost hunting party," I say. "A real ghost hunting party can only happen if there is a real ghost around. And I am pretty sure our ghost is already gone." Then I make my voice into a very soft, soft, soft whisper. "I will tell you a secret, Russ Robertson." He leans in very close. "A ghost did not draw that mustache on me. Someone else did. Someone who—"

Whoosh!

"HAILEY!" Maybelle says, popping up. "You cannot tell anyone about me! I told you!"

I sigh.

"Someone who?" Russ asks.

"No one," I say. "Never mind."

- - - - - - - - - - - - - - - - - - - -

After recess, we are allowed to change into our costumes! When we get back to our classroom, it looks like a party is going on! And that is because there *is* a party going on! It is time for our party about the countries of the world, and the whole room is filled with lots of good, good, good treats.

"Hello, Hailey," Antonio says. He is wearing a green and orange hat! It is so big it almost covers his whole face!

"Hello, down there!" I yell, looking under the bottom of that hat. "Are you under there, Antonio?"

"This," Antonio says, "is a *sombrero*. It is a Mexican hat. And my grandpa wears one all the time."

"And this," I say, "is a beret! They wear them in France sometimes."

"Cool!" Antonio says. And then I see Addie Jokobeck. She is over by the table of food, and she is setting out our tray of French fries. Mr. Jokobeck warmed them up in the cafeteria oven and then dropped them off. And then I feel very sad, sad, sad, like maybe I am going to cry.

"Let's eat some food," I say. I swallow big so that my tears don't come down my cheeks.

Antonio and I head over to the table that is filled with lots and lots and lots of good treats. Like our French fries. And Mexican quesadillas. And English truffles. And Thai noodles. Antonio and I put some food on tiny paper plates. Then we sit down.

"Antonio," I say while we eat. "Let's talk about our plan to dig a hole all the way to Antarctica."

"Okay," he says.

"It is going to be a very interesting adventure," I tell him. "First, we will—"

But I do not finish what I am saying. Because that is when I notice Addie sitting over in the corner. On the rug in the reading circle. All alone, by herself. She has her knees pulled all the way up, almost to her nose!

"Just one second," I say to Antonio. "I will be right back."

And I tiptoe over to where Addie is sitting.

"Oh, hello," I say, like I just happen to be walking by.

"Hello," Addie says. I wait for her to say, "Go away, you are not my friend anymore!" But she does not.

"What are you doing sitting over here?" I look at the weather calendar on the wall over Addie's head. I put a look on my face. One that says I just came over to check on the weather.

"Nothing," Addie says. "Just sitting."

"I like your costume," I say. This is supposed to be a very funny joke since Addie and I are wearing the exact same costume.

"Thank you," Addie says. I guess she is too upset to even laugh at jokes.

"Do you want to eat some French fries with me and Antonio?" I ask. "They are very crispy and very good."

And then Addie Jokobeck starts crying. She

bursts into tears just like I do when I have to spend the night places.

"Addie!" I say. "What's wrong?" I sit right down next to her. I am wearing a pair of black pants, and this morning my mom said, "Hailey, please be careful with these pants at school and try not to get them dirty." But this is an emergency!

"Ghoostt parrrshhhy," Addie says. Then she makes a big sniff. Ewwwww. I get Addie a tissue from the box on the windowsill.

"Nosh inviiissted," Addie says again. She is not making real words. Probably because she is too upset from all the crying. And then I realize why Addie is crying! It is because she has lost her friend and partner! Which is me! I am her friend and partner! And she is upset that we are fighting.

"Addie," I say, "I am very, very sorry I got you in trouble. And I think me and you should be friends again." I think about it some more. "I do not even care if you go to that ghost hunting party!" I think about it even some more. "*If* you promise never to tell Natalie any secrets that I tell you."

"NO," Addie says, and she makes another big sniff.

"No," I say. "What do you mean, no?" My heart feels like it is dropping into my shoes.

"I'm not crying because of that." Addie sniffs again.

And then Maybelle pops up right in front of me! She is still wearing that new green dress.

"Hailey!" Maybelle yells.

"Shh," I say out of the side of my mouth. "I am busy here."

"What?" Addie asks.

"Nothing," I say. "Now, you were just about to stop crying on account of how now we are friends again." I give her my biggest, best smile.

"HAILEY!" Maybelle screams. "This is very, very important!"

"But I'm not crying about you," Addie says. "I am crying about the…the ghost party!"

"What about it?" I ask.

"HAILEY!" Maybelle yells. And she pulls on my shirt.

"I. WAS. NOT. INVITED!" Addie is very

upset. She is almost crying and yelling at the same time. Although it is very hard to hear with all that shouting that Maybelle is doing. She is using a very outdoor sort of voice.

"How come?" I ask. I try to pull Maybelle's hands off my shirt without looking craze, craze, crazy.

"I don't know," Addie sniffs. "I think it is because I wouldn't tell Natalie if you were the one who threw away that list."

"That is the reason that you are not invited?" I ask. I start to have a very funny feeling in my stomach. And not a good one.

"Yes," Addie says. She is not crying anymore. Now she is just looking very sad.

"HAILEY!" Maybelle shrieks. "PLEASE!"

"Go away!" I yell.

"Okay," Addie says, and starts to get up.

"Sorry," I say. "Not you." I give Maybelle a mean look and *poof!* She disappears.

"Now," I say. "I think I know how I can fix this."

"You do?"

"Yes," I say. That funny, nervous feeling is back in my stomach. But I do not let it stop me. Because this time Natalie Brice has gone a little too far.

"How?" Addie wants to know.

"Follow me," I say. And then I march, march, march right up to where Natalie is sitting! In my seat! Right next to Antonio and they are probably making a plan to dig a hole all the way to Antarctica!

"Excuse me, Natalie," I say very politely. I tap, tap, tap her on the shoulder.

"Move your feet, lose your seat," she says. And then she turns back to eating her food.

"I do not want my seat," I say. "I want you to let Addie go to your party, please." I put a big smile on my face just in case

Natalie Brice feels like maybe being a little nice to me.

"No," Natalie says. And then she takes a big bite of one of the French fries on her plate. "Eww," she says. "These are not very good."

"That is a lie and you know it," I say. I start to feel like maybe I want to have a tantrum. "Those French fries are delicious!"

"No," Natalie says, "they are not."

So then I decide that enough is enough. "Oh, Natalie," I say. "A ghost did not throw away that list after all." I take a deep breath and get ready to be in trouble. "I did."

Natalie looks very surprised, like she cannot believe it. Her eyebrows are going up and down and her mouth drops all the way open.

"So," I say. "It is time to cancel that ghost hunting party, because there is no ghost." I smile again. "It was me, Hailey Twitch, who was causing all those problems."

Natalie is still very shocked.

"I am still going to have that party," she says.

"But no ghost hunting?" Antonio asks. He looks like he thinks that party might not be so fun after all.

"No, but we can play in my tree house," Natalie says.

"I already did that," Antonio tells her.

"Me too," says Megan Miller.

"Me too," says Russ Robertson.

"So I guess that party is not going on," Addie says from behind me. I turn around and give her a high five.

"These French fries are good," Antonio says. He puts three whole fries in his mouth at the same time.

"And if you are very lucky, they are good for a food fight," I tell him.

But before we can talk about this fabulous idea, there is one more thing that has to be done. I tiptoe up to the front of the room where Miss Stephanie is serving up some Chinese soup.

"Miss Stephanie?" I say politely. I stand very tall and quiet.

"Yes, Hailey?" Miss Stephanie says. She is dressed up like the Statue of Liberty for the party.

"I need to tell you that I threw that list of

partners in the garbage." I look down at my shoes and feel very, very sad.

"Hailey, is that true?" Miss Stephanie asks.

I want to say no. Because I did not throw that list in the garbage, Maybelle did. But then I see Natalie and she still looks mad, mad, mad. And I know that if I do not take the blame, Natalie will tell on me.

And so I say, "Yes, Miss Stephanie, I did throw that list in the garbage."

"That wasn't nice, Hailey," she says. "You know that is against the rules."

"I know," I say. "I am very sorry and it will not happen again." I try to look very sorry about my rule breaking. But I know what is going to happen now. I am going to get a punishment. And it will be to leave our party.

But Miss Stephanie only says, "We will talk about this later, Hailey." And I am not sure, but I think she might be smiling.

She is going to let me stay at the party! "Will we have to," I ask, crossing my fingers, "tell my parents about this?"

"I don't think so," Miss Stephanie says. "I am very happy you came out and admitted what you did. It is very grown up. But please be on your best behavior from now on."

Yay! This is turning into the best day ever! I go over to a new table and sit down with Addie Jokobeck.

"Have you ever heard about a plan to dig a hole all the way to Antarctica?" I ask her.

"No," she says, "but that sounds like a very fun adventure."

I give Addie Jokobeck a very, very big smile. And she gives me one too. And I feel very hap, hap, happy!

"Thank you, Hailey," Addie says. She takes a bite of a very delicious-looking cupcake.

"You're welcome," I say. And then I think

about something. "Addie," I say, "I am sorry if I was mean to you about being friends with Natalie Brice." I take another French fry off my plate. "Even if she is a mean one. And I am sorry if I got you in trouble."

"It's okay," Addie says. "I know you didn't mean it."

"Can we sit with you?" Antonio Fuerte asks. He is standing by our table with Russ Robertson.

"Yes," I say. I turn back to Addie. "I think it is okay for us to have other friends."

"Yes," she says, "I think you are right."

And then me and Russ and Addie and Antonio all talk about how to dig a big hole to Antarctica.

Chapter Eleven

Mr. Tuttle and the Department of Magic

We are just getting to the good part about digging the hole and figuring out the shovels when Maybelle poofs right back up!

"HAILEY!" she says. "I NEED YOU RIGHT NOW!"

"No," I whisper.

"YES," she says. And then I notice she is all done up. She is wearing a new purple dress and neon pink shoes. I will have to ask Kaitlyn about that, because I do not think it matches.

"I cannot," I say. "I am already on thin ice here." Being on thin ice is when you are almost in trouble but not quite.

"Hailey, PLEASE," she says. "This is a very big emergency." And then I realize she means business.

"Excuse me, please," I say politely to Russ and Addie. And then I ask Miss Stephanie if I can please go to the bathroom.

"What?" I ask Maybelle once we are in the bathroom. I check all the stalls first to make sure no one is listening in. Like being a spy.

"We have a bit of a...problem," she says. And then poof! Another person poofs up! A little man with a mustache and a weird tan coat and big huge glasses!

"Hello," he says. "Are you Hailey Twitch?"

"Well," I say. I think about this. "That depends on whether or not she's in trouble."

"No," he says, "she's not in trouble."

"Then, yes," I say, "I am Hailey Twitch." And then I remember my manners. "I am pleased to meet you, Mr....?"

"Mr. Tuttle," he says. "Department of Magic."

"Department of Magic?" I ask. "Magic does not sound like it should have a department." A department sounds very serious and dark. Which is not very fun at all.

"No time for small talk," he says. Then he pushes up his glasses and looks at me kind of seriously. "We need," he says, "to talk about Maybelle. And it is *very* important."

Yikes. I am not so sure about this. Usually when a grown-up wants to have an important talk with you, it means it might be time for a punishment. I think it over very, very careful.

"Fine," I say, "I will talk to you about Maybelle, Mr. Tuttle. But make it quick please, since there is a very big party going on in the other room."

Mr. Tuttle looks down at his clipboard. And then he starts to tell me that important thing about Maybelle. I listen real close, and my jaw goes drop, drop, dropping right to the ground. As if getting a magic sprite wasn't enough for one girl to handle! How am I going to deal with this? I guess we will just have to wait and see...

Acknowledgments

Thank you so, so much to:

Daniel Ehrenhaft, my fab editor, for taking over with such enthusiasm, and making this book a million times better.

Lyron Bennett for believing in Hailey from the beginning.

Dominique Raccah, Kelly Barrales-Saylor, and everyone at Sourcebooks for all their hard work.

Suzanne Beaky for bringing Hailey and Maybelle alive and making them look better than I ever could have imagined.

My mom, my dad, and my sisters for all their support.

Jennifer Lynn Barnes, Jackson Pearce, Jessica Burkhart, Mandy Hubbard, and Diana

Peterfreund for answering my "OMG, I'm freaking out" email.

Kevin Cregg, Scott Neumyer, and Jodi Yanarella for just being great.

And most of all, my husband, Aaron, for everything.

Hailey Twitch Saves the Play

I have a very big secret. And that secret is that I have a magic sprite. Her name is Maybelle and she has long sparkly blond hair and beautiful glittery wings and she came flying out of my magic castle last week. She lived in there for two hundred whole years and I, Hailey Twitch, am the only one who can see her.

There are some good things about having a magic sprite, and some bad things. The good things are that no one else can see her. So it is like a big secret you have to keep with yourself! The bad things are that sometimes your sprite might get you into trouble for something that you did not even do. Like when Maybelle used a marker to draw on skin and my teacher Miss Stephanie thought it was all my fault.

Also Maybelle cannot even do any good magic. She got her magic taken away because she was not fun, like a sprite should be. But she is working on it. Which is why I am in the bathroom at school right now, even though we are right in the middle of having a Countries of the World Party in room four, Ms. Stephanie's second grade. I had to leave that very fun, fun, fun party because Mr. Tuttle is in the girls' bathroom.

Mr. Tuttle is the head of the Department of Magic. And he is here to make sure that Maybelle is getting fun. Otherwise she will not be able to get her magic back.

"Now," Mr. Tuttle says. "We have to talk about Maybelle. It is very important."

Mr. Tuttle is a little scary. He is just as tall as me with a very big belly. Also he has big black glasses and a clipboard. A clipboard is where grownups write bad things about you. Like if you start being bad and need a good punishment. Unfortunately I know all about that.

"I guess so," I say. I wonder if I can tell him to hurry up, please. I am missing the party where Antonio Fuerte is maybe going to do a special Mexican dance. Antonio Fuerte is one of my friends. He has black hair and black eyes and today he is wearing a sombrero.

"Maybelle needs to work on having more fun," Mr. Tuttle says. He looks at me over his glasses. His eyes are very big under there. "And so you, Hailey, are going to be in charge of her."

"You mean…you mean like the boss of her?" I say. Suddenly, I am paying very good attention! This is very happy news, even better than being at the party! I love being the boss of people! And now I am the boss of my very own magic sprite! It is official.

"Yes," Mr. Tuttle says.

Maybelle just sits there on the sink. She is getting her new sparkly green dress all dirty on the bottom. And she looks very nervous. I give her a little pat on the back. But she does not seem too cheered up.

"Now, one of the things Maybelle must do in order to become more fun," Mr. Tuttle says, "is to make one new friend."

"One new friend?" I try not to seem like a snob about this. But making one new friend is very easy. I just made one new friend named Addie Jokobeck. "Are you sure that's all?"

"Yes," Mr. Tuttle replies. "And you will report back to me on how she is doing."

"Yes, sir!" I give Mr. Tuttle a salute just like they do in the army. "How should I report to you?" I ask. "Should I maybe give Maybelle a report card?"

"No," Mr. Tuttle says.

"Should I give her a student of the month for friendship if she is good?"

"No," Mr. Tuttle says.

"How about if I—"

"Hailey!" Mr. Tuttle says. "Please. I will come back in one week and you will tell me if Maybelle has made a new friend. That is all." And then there is a little blue flash like lightning and Mr. Tuttle is gone. Well. I guess that means I will not be getting my very own clipboard. But oh well. I am still the boss of Maybelle!

"Oh no!" Maybelle says from the edge of the sink.

"I do not think it is too clean in there," I tell her. "One time I saw Megan Miller have a big runny nose in that sink."

"How am I going to make a friend?"

Maybelle asks. She looks like maybe she is going to cry any minute. "I cannot make a friend! I am doomed."

"You are not doomed," I say. "Don't worry. You can make a friend. I will help you." I give her my most best smile. "It will be very easy."

About the Author

Lauren Barnholdt loves reading, writing, and anything pink and sparkly. She's never had a magic sprite, but she *does* have four guinea pigs. She lives outside of Boston with her husband. Visit her website and say hello at www.laurenbarnholdt.com.

About the Illustrator

Suzanne Beaky grew up in Gahanna, Ohio, and studied illustration at Columbus College of Art and Design. Her expressive illustrations are commissioned by children's book, magazine, and educational publishers worldwide. She now lives with her husband and their cats, who insist on sitting in her lap while she works and often step in her paint, in Kirksville, Missouri.